The Fart Book

The Adventures of Milo Snotrocket

J.B. O'Neil

Published by J.J. Fast Publishing LLC

The Fart Book

Table of Contents

For my son Joe, who loves to laugh about completely disgusting stuff like boogers, farts, barf, poop, snot, and pee...Enjoy!

FREE BONUS – Ninja Farts Audiobook

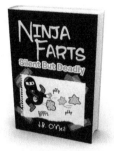

Hey gang...If you'd like to listen to the hilarious audiobook version of my fart-tastic new book "Ninja Farts – Silent But Deadly," you can download it for free for a limited time by going online and copying this link: http://funnyfarts.net/

Enjoy!

The Sideshot

If you're one of those lucky people with a natural talent for butt whistling, as we suspect you are, or if you fancy yourself the maestro of a one-kid gassy grumbling orchestra, you're probably familiar with the classic sideshot. It happens to be the simplest, easiest move in the book. Even backdoor breezy dabblers can do it. And whether you're an amateur or a super advanced expert bean blower, you've probably noticed it before. Maybe it was the old man sitting on a park bench feeding the pigeons or the kid who sits in front of you at school.

Anyone can perfect the two-step sideshot. Step one is just prep work, setting the scene for maximum airflow. All you have to do is tilt one hip to the side like you're about to tip over, keep your balance and hold on for step two, the bottom belch, faster than a speeding spit wad.

For a nice clean shot, try a 45-degree angle. For sneaky situations--they won't know what hit 'em!-- go for something more acute (a.k.a. the one-cheek sneak). We guarantee you won't tear your pants with this one. It's a good sitting exercise too and it's how I met one of my best friends, Farty McPhee. I spotted him doing the sideshot on the seesaw (not as easy as you'd imagine) and knew I'd found my partner in slime.

The Skipping Stone

On a gorgeous spring day when the grass is swaying and the birds are singing in the trees and you feel like having a picnic in the park or taking a nap by a lake in perfect weather, you might hear a little grumbling, feel some gaseous energy baking brownies in your tummy. And if no one is around except the frogs in the bushes and the slugs dragging their slimy shells through the grass, all one with nature, you'll take a deep breath and know it's time for the skipping stone.

Amidst all the outdoor sights and sounds and smells, you'll want to throw in your own airy chimes. Go ahead. Clench and release. It might sound like a stone skipping on water.

Like hoppity - hoppity - hop - kerplunk! Or more like birdsong. Chirp - chirp - chirp - tweeeeeeeet.

The key to the skipping stone is to let it sing. Listen to your butt chimes work their magic. It's all natural. This windy ripple fart will make you feel much closer to Mother Nature.

Morse Code

A top-secret farting method for super sleuths and spies, this one is not for the amateur, we assure you. This is serious stuff only for the flatulent elite. Learning to intercept and send your own Morse Code messages vapor-style is like joining a secret club. It isn't easy. It'll take a whole lot of practice to get it right, but when you do, you'll be able to send messages to your friends and fellow Morse belchers without ever getting caught.

For example, *Toot-toooot-tooooot. Toot! Too-toot. Toot-tooooooo-toot. Toooot-too-toot* is "Weird" in fartspeak.

Practice this with someone you share secrets and adventures with. (My buddy Farty McPhee and I are getting pretty good at this.) You'll be able to have entire conversations--though you'll want to keep them short--

while everyone around you cluelessly wrinkles their noses.

The best part is that all evidence of the message dissolves into thin air, vanishes into unknowing nostrils without a trace.

The Rocket Ship

It goes by many names. Rocket ship, seat blaster, vapor volcano. Only one thing is certain: it'll have you flying out of your chair. Forget gravity. Forget roller coasters. Forget tornadoes. Twisters will seem like dust mites compared to this rocket-shooting methane canon fart. The rocket ship is strong enough to send you floating through space on a powerful gas propeller, although most of the time you'll stop short of the ozone layer.

The single recorded incident that broke the atmospheric barrier was by an unusually hungry boy of eight who was obsessed with chili, black beans and burritos. After his fifth meal of the day and about a hundred burps, he closed his eyes, rubbed his belly and was suddenly launched up, up and away until he was completely out of sight. If you look up at the sky on cloudless nights, you can still see his sombrero floating in space.

Parents, teachers, cafeterias and taquerias agreed on a one-burrito-per-day-per-kid rule after that, which is really a shame if you think about it. Still, it hasn't stopped the rocket ship from making an appearance now and then, although usually it makes smaller flights. Mostly domestic. It might send you blasting up from your tree house to a nearby water tower or the Empire State Building in New York. When you feel it rumbling in your tummy, ready to take off, act quickly and strap a parachute onto your back 'cause you're in for the ride of your life. If you're an exceptional farter, you might even get across the Pacific. Say goodbye earth and hey sky, hello world

The Scream

Have you ever woken up in the middle of the night with an anxious feeling? As though you were jarred awake by a ghost whizzing by or an insect buzzing around in your room while you slept? Or a bad dream with creepy high-pitched voices? Don't be afraid.

Chances are it was just the scream fart, a long, loud extremely high-pitched bottom whistle. It can be pretty alarming and doesn't sound anything like your average bottom burp. This one belongs in a horror movie for its blood-curdling frequency.

It'll make your skin crawl. To ghosts, it sounds like nails on a chalkboard. If you want to scare away potential monsters lurking in the shadows, you may want to let out an ear-piercing scream fart. It's also a good weapon against bullies and boring teachers. When in danger or just to get out of the classroom for a minute, spice things up with a screamer.

The Sputter

When a car's engine sputters out, you take it to the garage so the mechanic can have a look. When a fart sputters out, you give your compliments to the chef. In some cultures, the polite thing to do is burp after a meal.

In the same way, according to the Etiquette Manual published by the Society of Fart Enthusiasts, of which I am a lifetime member (You should join us!) farting can be seen as a similar gesture of appreciation.

It's like applause for a job well done, a meal enjoyed. And like all applause, it fades away. Sadly, even the lingering scent of a grateful fart must fade.

But the sputter always starts strong, with great thunderous bugle sounds of appreciation. The rest is just like the chuckles and hiccups after uproarious bouts of laughter.

The Explosion

Ever felt the earth rumbling beneath your feet? You probably thought it was an earthquake. With all the alarming news on television about volcanoes erupting and groundbreaking tremors, the thought of another natural disaster would naturally cross your mind. Not to worry. Most of the time the rumbling is just the beginning of an enormous, gargantuan, humongous, echoing belch. Like thunder before a storm, before it really starts to pour, you'll hear a steady thunderous rumbling.

First your bottom starts to tingle, then your tummy starts to grumble and your toes start to tremble and your chair or the floor under your feet begins to groan. That's when you know a big one is coming. You'll want to brace yourself, but there's nowhere to hide. You'll want to run for the bathroom, but it's too far away and no four walls can contain this huge explosion. The expert's advice is just to let it happen. Plant both feet on the ground, get into superhero stance, and unleash that earth-shaking whopper of gas.

Classical Farts

I bet you know someone who loves classical music. Maybe the shy girl at school is becoming a virtuoso with the violin, or your sister dreams of being a soprano in a world-famous choir. Maybe your dad hums along to a symphony while he shaves in the morning, or your grandma listens to opera in the evening. Most people are familiar with at least a little bit of classic music even though it's not nearly as popular these days as, well, pop music. The thing that makes it classical though is its timeless appeal.

Anyone who's heard the vibrato fart would agree. People who've heard the intense beauty of the musical scales in the acoustic style of musical farting will never forget the ear candy. The Vibrato is definitely one of the more artistic ways to break wind. You might even want to practice so you can play your grandma a little ditty the next time she visits.

Popcorn Farting

No, you don't need a microwave the size of a refrigerator to add the popcorn variety to your list of gassy triumphs. All you need is great butt reflexes and a whole lot of wind. The popcorn variety requires some stamina because it always comes in a series, a sequence of bottom pops, so to speak.

Have you ever heard of just one kernel of popcorn popping? It's unthinkable.

So if you have the butt reflexes ready and it's a go for the whole lot of wind, then you might be able to pull this one off. Also known as the machine gun, it's one of the most fun and impressive fart techniques. Use it to play cops and robbers, with real stink guns, or to drive away skunks and other creatures you don't want rummaging through your trash or sneaking around in your backyard.

Musical Farts

Like to dance but can't find the perfect song for your next routine? Find a microphone and recorder and string a variety of farts together to make your own rhythm. You might be able to come up with some great beats and everyone who sees your act will be wondering where that amazing music is from. Drum roll--no, butt cheeks--please!

Farts as Weapons

You're a good kid. You wouldn't hurt a fly. Or maybe just a fly, and the occasional slug. But how do you get back at the school bully while maintaining your squeaky clean reputation for being an all-around awesome peace-keeping kid? The fart is the answer. You'll have to be an avid collector to see this plan through, but it'll be well worth it. All you have to do is gather a bunch of different sized jars to keep your farts in. Keep them airtight and sealed and carry one in your backpack in case of emergencies. If you find yourself in a sticky situation with the school bully, just take the jar out and unleash the magic poo perfume. You'll have him either running away in disgust or completely stunned into submission by your smelly potion.

The Strong Silent Type

Some women say they prefer this type but if you test this one out with the girls at school, you'll soon figure out this just isn't the case. Not with the strong silent fart, anyway. This is known for its extremely strong won't-hear-it-coming odor, which just sneaks up on you with no warning whatsoever.

Other farts announce their stinkiness with a long honk or a soft squeak at least, but the strong silent type just fills the room with its smelly presence. It travels fast too, and the source has every opportunity to keep quiet and leave everyone to wonder where that stink bomb came from. Often the strong silent type's origins will remain a mystery forever to those unlucky enough to smell it.

This is the best fart for people who like to multitask. You can be chatting with someone at a party or helping your mom do her shopping. You can do these things all while the strong silent type brews a stinky one. And when you let it out, you just wrinkle your nose, shake your head and ask the person beside you if it was them.

The Rotten Egg Cloud

Whether it floats into the room from a loudly booming, extremely soft, or completely quiet backdoor breeze, the rotten egg cloud is an unmistakable fart phenomenon. Why? Because it smells like rotten eggs and milk gone bad, literally *reeks* of expired dairy. But the milky sour stench is not the most distinct feature of this particular fart. It's the way it moves and tickles the nostrils of everyone who gets in its path.

It's called a cloud because of its sheer overwhelming presence, following the farter and its other unwitting victims around like a rain cloud looming dangerously close to the ground. You definitely don't want to get caught in it like a plane gets caught in a cloud of turbulence. Even expert bottom blasters pinch their noses for this one. It sticks to your clothes for hours, there's no avoiding it. The only thing you can do is hold your breath.

Poo Perfume

Wear this rare human concoction and you'll be sure to attract the neighborhood oddballs and dirty looks from passing strangers. One whiff will send the average person reeling, scampering around for a bouquet of roses or a bowl of potpourri to stick their heads into.

Don't wear too much of it unless you want people to grimace and faint at the first whiff of you. While it's a fact that not everyone can pull off this statement scent, it's definitely popular in some circles. It's in pretty high demand because the bottling process requires a lot of time and care, and only the stinkiest, smelliest farts are used to extract the essence of poo perfume. The President of the Society of Fart Enthusiasts wears just a hint of it--it's his signature scent--to our all-important quarterly meetings where we discuss cutting-edge farting techniques and breakthroughs in backfiring vapors. See Chapter 11 for additional uses.

The Party Pooper

This festive stink torpedo goes off like a firework and is perfect for large gatherings. Make sure your grandma has her smelling salts before you unleash this one. The Party Pooper is not for the faint of heart and the unprepared. It'll catch you off guard right as you're bobbing your head to a catchy tune, busting a move on the dance floor or talking to a girl at the soda fountain. This is one party favor that never goes unnoticed.

Loud and stinky with perfect timing. Sure to turn heads and make the farter the life of the party or the butt of jokes, especially if the party pooper surprises everyone in the middle of musical chairs (when the music stops) or a game of Twister (which was a really popular party game grown-ups used to play when they were kids).

At your next birthday celebration, consider being the belcher boy. Who needs a clown? The party pooper will knock the party hats off your guests.

The Red Alert

Have you ever been in the middle of a scene in the school play or stuck in the car on the highway miles from the nearest rest stop and felt the red alert well up inside you? It grumble-grumbles and chews at your stomach and you know it'll go off any second. And it does, like a long loud siren.

Just when it's especially important to keep your pants buttoned, the red alert means business: get to the bathroom fast before you're reduced to a whimpering baby in need of a diaper-changing. It's always at the worst time too, which is why it's so urgent. You'll wish your mom hadn't made you eat those prunes with your cereal that morning.

This threatening warning fart will make you feel like good old fiber is not your friend. The best thing to do is slip away, look around and make a mad dash for the closest toilet.

The Bottle Cap

The Bottle Cap, which pops when you twist to the right, is a personal favorite for dancers and hula-hoop champions alike. It's hard to do it perfectly but with a little practice you'll be able to bust this move and blast those fart fumes to the rhythm in no time.

The first step to doing this right is putting on some good music. "Do the Twist" and "Twist and Shout" used to be the Bottle Cap anthems--they've been farting this way since before our grandparents were born--but anything upbeat, jiggly, wiggly and fun will do as long as it's pop music.

Pop is key to the Bottle Cap boogie. So do some stretching and spread your arms, jump around and throw your hands in the air, wiggle your fingers and swish your feet. Then twist! Elbows in and knees a little bent, side to side like a spinning top. And pop! That's the bottle cap fart. A loud popcorn sort of pop, with a swish and a fizzle, the darling of the dance floor that comes out when you wiggle.

The Rattle Snake

The Rattle Snake fart is pure noxious stink. It'll make you cover your nose and say "Pee-yoo! Is that poison? Is that rotten eggs or a science lab accident? Did something crawl under the floorboards and die?"

At our last all-important meeting, the President of the Society of Fart Enthusiasts did a demonstration of the Rattle Snake fart and the sound of his sputtering vapor venom lasted all of eight minutes, a world record. The smell stuck around much longer and we got complaints from the maintenance crew.

I wanted to try it out myself and after several attempts and a lot of gas passed, I finally got it right. It drove my mom crazy though. She kept looking out the window and under the furniture looking for the source, worried she might have to call an exterminator. When she found out it was me, she said, "Milo Snotrocket, if you're going to fart like a rattle snake, please do it in the yard."

The Stirrer

The stirrer always gives me a stomachache. It usually starts at night when you're watching a documentary on the Discovery channel about whirlpools or tornadoes or something equally stirring. Your stomach takes the hint and something starts to brew its own little twister in your tummy, putting everything you ate that day-- peanut butter, cheese, pretzels, mom's meatloaf-- through a gassy blender.

To make matters worse, when you go to bed with a stirrer fart in you, you have dreams of blenders blending really funky things like mushy bananas with insect wings and pickle juice or expired milk, ketchup globs and celery sticks--things you do not want rolling around in your stomach. To top it all of, the next morning, I watched my mom make one of her all-natural healthy smoothies--carotene-packed carrot with a spoonful of cod liver oil for a glowing complexion--I thought I would hurl all over the breakfast spread. The stirrer was swirling around in my stomach, threatening to let itself out when I did a quick sideshot, unleashed that gassy stirrer and averted the disaster.

The Cough Cover-Up

If you don't want anyone to hear your fart, distract them with a really loud cough to mask it. The art of the cover up can really come in handy. At movie theater or restaurants, for example.

I've sort of earned a reputation for being a gooey booger boy and fart master at school so my homeroom teacher has asked me to keep my show tune--meant to impress-- farts down to one a day. But there's no limit to how many times I can cough! Or sneeze. Or burp.

You'd be amazed at how much gas an eight-year-old boy can unleash on the world. What really gets to me though is that I can't always claim my proudest farts, my cafeteria slush-inspired, stinkiest, light-a-match-to-see- a-mega-explosion farts that happen to come to me in the classroom after lunch, usually when I'm working on multiplication tables.

Of course, even with the cough cover-up, when the vinegar-scented gas starts spreading around the room people look at me with both disgust and admiration.

The After Fart

The After Fart is the curtain call of farts, the encore, and the hand shooting up from the grave in the last scene of that creepy horror film. It is a spine-tingling surprise and at the same time extremely revolting. As if my rotten eggs soaked in vinegar whiff-and-sniff cloud were not enough, the after fart tops it off with a loud walloping stink steamer. The exclamation point of farts!

I've heard that the greatest speakers in history have used them to make a point so when I was running for class president and had to make a speech I made sure to blow some huge after farts after my best points.

"Whoopee cushions for everyone!" Plooooot.

"No school on Saturdays!" Double prooooot.

They also come with a smell you won't forget--a mix of poo and dirty gym socks, pretty overpowering. If you like to have the last laugh or the last word, the after fart would be your pooplet puff of choice. Make it last.

The Duet

The duet comes in two forms. If you're a one-kid show, you can match your toilet tune with a froggy burp. Try to get some phlegm in there too to add a croaky texture to the piece. You'll come up with a thunder pants sort of harmony, a really unique sound, in my opinion.

That's why I was puzzled when I suggested it to my music teacher as a solo for our Christmas program and she only laughed and gave me a pat on the head. I was being serious! I would've eaten all my vegetables the week of the performance to get my frowsiest, funkiest, greenest gas ready to blow.

Anyway, I wasn't too disappointed because my solo act is just not as polished as my two-kid duet featuring my good friend and farting rival-in-volume-and-stinkiness

Farty McPhee. The Duet is our signature rhythm-and-stench jig, very popular with the playground crowd. He does the fart-and-burp and I do the fart-and-fake-sneeze. Sometimes we throw in some sweat-powered armpit horns too but our trouser trumpets always steal the show for their stinkiness.

The Squirt

The squirt fart is my mom's least favorite (and she's not a huge fan of my gas-passing passion at it is) but the squirt is monumental, a real hall of famer according to the Society of Fart Enthusiasts, not just because it takes the stench scale to ultimate heights but because of the color it brings to your life. Call it the pant stainer, the mud duck, gravy pants, expanding odor balloon.

It is nose death and definitely leaves a mark. Not for the pop-a-fluffy dabbler, this stink biscuit is for serious farters only. I mean the gravest gas attackers on the planet and possibly other planets too. If an alien ever lands on earth and wants to learn inside squirt secrets, I'm not even sure I could explain the gooey gift, the tiny liquid jewel-drops of human creation. If he really insisted and promised not to spread it around the galaxy, I'd give him the tip.

The tip is: prunes and a gallon of milk. Squirts galore.

The Racer

The racer revs up and makes a vrrrooooom sound and basically just sets your pants on fire with speed. I use it once in a while when I'm really late for school. It makes me go a whole lot faster than our dinky old school bus ever could. It's not that I become a blur to the kids on the bus who aren't as flatulently blessed as I am. I can accelerate just enough with the gas guzzling seat of my pants to wave at them as I whizz past.

"How does he do it?" they wonder. "Does he have a built-in engine on his backpack?" "Is he on lightning-powered roller blades?" Ha! None of them will guess that I've just let the racer fart rip up the streets with its smooth poo propeller and smoothest velocity.

That's why I'm never late for school, and I can watch all the other kids pile into the room, grumbling and sniffing and trying to put a finger on my air bagels. The mystery of my speed remains.

The Sonic Boom

A really memorable one, it will horrify everyone within a fifty-mile radius. I saved the sonic boom for last because it's one of the top secret weapons being developed by an astronomically top secret team of scientists commissioned by the Society of Fart Enthusiasts.

In fact, most of our profits from selling poo perfume door-to-door go to the research fund for the Sonic Boom. It's the ultimate defense weapon not just for the SFE, but society at large, possibly the entire nation.

Due to the confidential nature of the project, however, this is all I can disclose: It involves airtight capsules that preserve and amplify the stinkiest farts from far and wide and some of the most isolated regions in the world. The amplification technology will make the sonic boom our greatest safeguard against dangers I'm not at liberty to speak of (hint: extraterrestrial threats).

And guess what?

I've made a special contribution to the project: my very own super stinky signature Snotrocket zinger, a specimen as disgusting as anything.

Elevator Farting

Do you know what claustrophobia is? It means an extreme or irrational fear of confined spaces. While I have no problem with tight spaces--one of my long-term goals is to dig a tunnel and crawl all the way to China in it--some people are really terrified by the thought of being closed in. And apparently a fart inside an elevator is a claustrophobic person's worst nightmare.

I had to learn this the hard way. I was visiting my dad at his office and riding the elevator up to 87th floor of his building when I started to feel a major bubble of poop gas about to burst, so naturally I let it rip. No use holding in a perfectly good stink torpedo.

What I didn't know was that the man I was sharing the elevator with was borderline claustrophobic and my dripping rotten egg cloud drove him over the edge. His eyes nearly popped out of his head and, believe me, you do not want to see what the back of someone's eyeballs look like, veiny and glazed with a shiny goo. He started clawing at the elevator buttons, stumbled out on the next floor and took the stairs I think.

Airplane Farts

I tell you, nothing feels better than releasing a
gargantuan goose bump-inducing gas blast at forty
thousand feet above sea level. The problem is the other
passengers won't enjoy it half as much as you do. In fact,
there will be no pleasure on their end. Just a lot of
hyperventilating and deep breathing into the motion
sickness bags tucked behind the safety information
sheet.

Really, they should have a figure on that sheet that tells
people how to react when sudden bouts of belch
balloons threaten to blast you right out of the aircraft.
That's what happened to me. So I let it rip. What
followed was the rotten egg cloud I've grown so fond of,
and some gagging noises down the aisle. Ooops. Farty
McPhee flew to Tallahassee last winter and said he saw

my picture on the safety information sheet. There was a fairly accurate rendering of a boy with the unmistakably charming Milo Snotrocket snicker letting out a humongous poop puff, out of which end you know, and a large red X over the scene. Ooops. I never thought my awesome thunder pants would actually inspire a change in airline security policy. I'll never be able to fly anonymously again. This, my friends, is called notoriety, but it'll get me into the hall of fame at the Society of Fart Enthusiasts. Smell that!

MORE FUNNY FARTS...

If you laughed really hard at The Fart Book, I know you'll love these other stinky bestselling books by J.B. O'Neil (for kids of *all* ages!)

http://jjsnip.com/booger-fart-books

Silent but Deadly...As a Ninja Should Be!

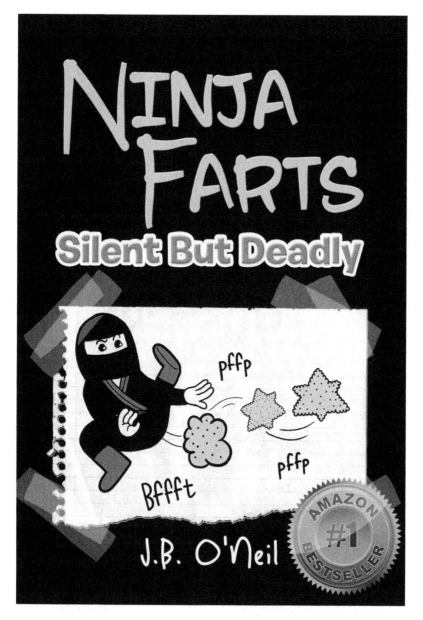

http://jjsnip.com/ninja-farts-book

Did you know cavemen farted?

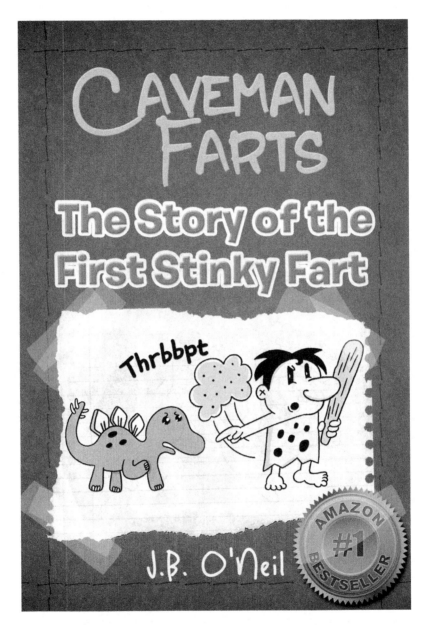

http://jjsnip.com/caveman-farts

A long time ago, in a galaxy fart, fart away...

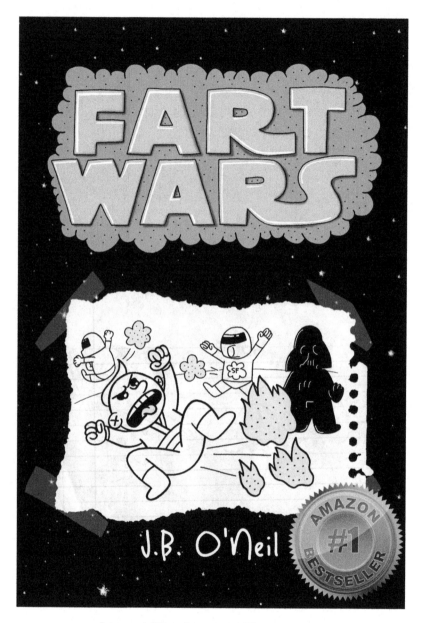

http://jjsnip.com/fart-wars

Think twice before you blame the dog!

http://jjsnip.com/dog-farts

And check out my new series, the

Family Avengers!

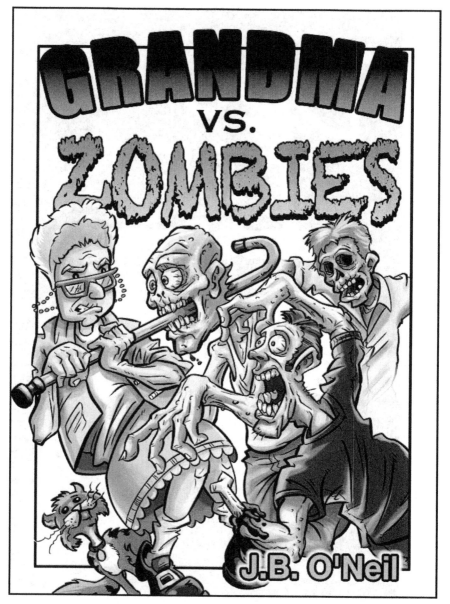

http://jjsnip.com/gvz

70

Made in the USA
Middletown, DE
04 February 2021

33119668R00040

From #1 Bestselling Children's Book Author J.B. O'Neil comes: The Fart Book. Here's what people are saying about this hilarious illustrated book for kids of all ages:

"I downloaded th[...]ed with my 6 years old daughter. I started rea[...]d to ask my hubby to continue reading with her! Both dad and daughter had quality times reading through the chapters and had lots of loud laughs. Thank you J.B O'Neil!"

"My 9-year-old son & I read this together and he laughed and laughed."

"Highly recommend!...No more dilemmas in what to buy for future presents for him or my friends children - would definitely buy more from this author in this series- so please write some more!"

Your copy of "The Fart Book" also includes a FREE audio-book edition of J.B. O'Neil's bestselling book "Ninja Farts." Look inside for more information. Enjoy!

ISBN 9781484926475

90000

9 781484 926475